ACTIVISM IN ACTION
······· A HISTORY™ ·······

THE FIGHT FOR
CIVIL RIGHTS

AVERY ELIZABETH HURT

Rosen
YA™
New York

To my adopted home, Birmingham, Alabama, where people marched in the streets, sat at lunch counters, and stood firm in their resolve—a place where people are still working to right wrongs and make the world a better place. I am both proud and humbled to call you home.

Published in 2020 by The Rosen Publishing Group, Inc.
29 East 21st Street, New York, NY 10010

First Edition

Library of Congress Cataloging-in-Publication Data

Names: Hurt, Avery Elizabeth, author.
Title: The fight for civil rights / Avery Elizabeth Hurt.
Description: New York : Rosen YA, 2020 | Series: Activism in action: a history | Includes bibliographical references and index.
Identifiers: LCCN 2018010899| ISBN 9781508185413 (library bound) | ISBN 9781508185406 (pbk.)
Subjects: LCSH: African Americans—Civil rights—History—20th century—Juvenile literature. | Civil rights movements—United States—History—20th century—Juvenile literature. | United States—Race relations—Juvenile literature.
Classification: LCC E185.61 .H977 2020 | DDC 323.1196/0730904—dc23
LC record available at https://lccn.loc.gov/2018010899

Manufactured in China

On the cover: Courageous leaders, such as Dr. Martin Luther King Jr. (*top*), and nationwide movements, such as Black Lives Matter, help to inspire change in the fight for civil rights.

CONTENTS

INTRODUCTION

I n 1861, the United States was torn in two over the issue of slavery. The Union of the North wanted to end slavery, while the Confederacy of the South wanted the practice to continue. The nation endured a four-year civil war, and in 1865, slavery was abolished. In the years that followed, former slaves and their descendants were guaranteed full citizenship. Black men were even given the right to vote. Things looked promising, until the nation systematically began denying them their civil rights. A system of racial discrimination in the South, and less systematic but no less damaging discrimination in the North, kept blacks from enjoying the rights, privileges, and opportunities that white citizens took for granted.

African Americans were not only denied their civil rights but were often terrorized. If a black person dared to challenge or even question the status quo, he or she was likely to be beaten or murdered. It was not uncommon for mobs of angry white men to hang a black person for a minor offense or for no reason at all. A white person who committed a similar crime was rarely punished. As the years went on, blacks began to organize and take steps

In 1968, Students at Columbia University listen as speakers from the Students for a Democratic Society speak out about civil rights.

to change the system. But real and lasting changes were few and far between.

In the middle of the twentieth century, things began to change. African Americans had had enough. Leaders such as Dr. Martin Luther King Jr., Rosa Parks, Bayard Rustin, Gloria Richardson, Ralph Abernathy, Fred Shuttlesworth, John Lewis, A. Philip Randolph, and many more took to the streets to make their voices heard.

Hundreds of thousands of people followed them, including schoolchildren and college students, men and women, the young and old.

The civil rights movement was one of the most effective social movements in history. Between the mid-1950s and the mid-1960s, civil rights activists in the United States challenged segregation in schools, public transportation, and public spaces—and won. They crashed through barriers for voting rights and forced the government to pass laws to provide equal job opportunities and end discrimination in the workplace. In a manner of speaking, they held up a mirror for the nation to look at its own hatred.

Activists achieved great strides in the civil rights movement by using nonviolent techniques of passive resistance. They didn't throw bombs, though bombs were thrown at them. They didn't burn down buildings, though many of their homes and churches were burned. They marched. They sang. They refused to leave when told to do so, and they refused to leave when sprayed with fire hoses. Activists marched in small towns and in big cities. They even marched up to the nation's capital. Every step, action, song, and refusal to give in changed a nation and its place in the world. The exciting and sometimes heartbreaking stories of these change makers portray them as full of courage, pride, and love—and ultimately triumphant, propelling the fight for civil rights.

CHAPTER ONE

THE LONG MARCH AHEAD

On March 7, 1965, six hundred demonstrators gathered on a chilly Sunday in Selma, Alabama. They planned to march to the state's capital, Montgomery, almost 50 miles (80 kilometers) away. Their goal was to highlight the need for laws that would protect the voting rights of African Americans. They also marched to commemorate the death of Jimmy Lee Jackson, who had been fatally shot by a state trooper a few weeks earlier. Jackson had been trying to protect his mother at a voter registration protest in Marion, Alabama.

Marchers set out on US Route 80, heading east toward Montgomery. The participating men, women, and children were hopeful, unarmed, and walking peacefully. Some were holding hands. Others were singing softly or talking quietly with fellow marchers. After six blocks, they reached the Edmund Pettus Bridge, which stretches across the Alabama River. On the other side of the bridge were state and local law enforcement officers, waiting for the peaceful demonstrators. Most of the officers were on foot. Some were on

People line the streets of Montgomery, Alabama, to watch the Selma to Montgomery marchers as they walk by in March 1965.

horseback. The activists paused for a moment and then began crossing the bridge. One of the march leaders, twenty-four-year-old John Lewis, suggested they pray. Word spread throughout the crowd, and prayers were said as they crossed the bridge. The police, however, attacked the peaceful demonstrators with clubs and tear gas. They rode their horses into the crowd, beating people with nightsticks and spraying them with tear gas. The police forced the marchers back across the bridge and back through Selma.

Seventeen people, including Lewis, were injured on what became known as Bloody Sunday.

ONCE MORE, WITH FEELING

Two days later, on March 9, fifteen hundred protesters headed out again from Selma toward the Edmund Pettus Bridge. This time, they were led by civil rights leader Dr. Martin Luther King Jr. National news shows had covered the story of Bloody Sunday, and the world was watching. Protesters did not intend to march all

The air fills with clouds of tear gas as Alabama state troopers, under orders from Governor George Wallace, attempt to disperse the marchers on Bloody Sunday.

the way to Montgomery but planned to walk to the Edmund Pettus Bridge, where Alabama state troopers had set up a barricade to keep them from crossing. Marchers did not confront the police. Instead, they approached the barricades, knelt, and prayed. They then turned around and walked back to Selma. In cities across the country, people held marches to show solidarity with the protesters in Alabama.

Meanwhile, civil rights leaders asked the courts for federal protection for the March to Montgomery. District Court judge Frank M. Johnson granted it, and on March 21, the protesters started marching again. This time, the Alabama National Guard protected them. They walked about 12 miles (19 km) a day, sleeping in fields along the side of the road at night, sometimes in rain and mud. By the time they reached the capital on March 25, the group had swelled to twenty-five thousand. People of all colors had come from around the country to join the march for the voting rights of African Americans.

In his speech that day in Montgomery, as transcribed on Stanford University's King Institute website, Dr. King said, "The confrontation of good and evil compressed in the tiny community of Selma generated the massive power to turn the whole nation to a new course." Indeed, it had. On March 17, President Lyndon B. Johnson submitted a bill to Congress that would protect the voting rights of all Americans. On August 6, he signed the Voting Rights Act of 1965 into law. The Selma marches were not the beginning of the struggle for civil rights for African Americans, but they were certainly key moments in a movement that was rapidly gaining momentum.

JIM CROW

Black people have been struggling to be treated fairly ever since they were brought to America as slaves. After the Civil War ended in 1865, the Thirteenth Amendment to the Constitution ended slavery. Three years later, the Fourteenth Amendment affirmed that blacks were citizens. The Fifteenth Amendment gave black men the right to vote in 1870. (Women, regardless of ethnicity, were denied the right to vote until the Nineteenth Amendment was ratified in 1920.) Even though these amendments became the law of the land, freed slaves and their descendants were rarely treated as citizens. They were often denied their civil right to vote. This suppression was especially bad in the proslavery states that had sided with the Confederacy in the Civil War.

Beginning in the 1800s, southern states began to pass laws and enact practices that became

On June 9, 1961, about one hundred African Americans walk through the streets of Memphis, Tennessee, and attempt to sit at department store lunch counters to protest the city's Jim Crow laws.

known as Jim Crow laws. Jim Crow was a common derogatory name for black men. Jim Crow laws demanded that all African Americans attend separate schools, eat in separate restaurants, and drink from separate water fountains. Signs across the Jim Crow South read "Whites Only," preventing black people from using the same restrooms, riding in the same part of trains and buses, or using the same libraries as white people. Blacks were expected to treat whites with respect, calling them "sir" or "ma'am" and "Mr." or "Mrs." White people, in contrast, called blacks by their first names, going as far as to call grown men "boy." It was humiliating for the black community. Plus, any violation of the Jim Crows laws meant that a black person could be beaten or worse. Not only were blacks segregated, they were also terrorized and victimized. In order to enforce this class system, mobs of white racists attacked and killed blacks, often by lynching.

Blacks were also prevented from voting, since southern states came up with ways to keep them from exercising that right. Election officials charged a poll tax before people could vote. Because most blacks were very poor, they often could not afford to pay the tax. People were also required to pass a test proving that they could read and write before being allowed to vote. Many blacks couldn't read, but even those who could had trouble with the tests. The questions were fiendishly difficult and often logically inconsistent. Sometimes the questions didn't make sense. On a Louisiana literacy test, as reproduced on the Open Culture website, one question instructed the test taker to "draw a line around the number or letter of this sentence." Another read, "In the space below, draw three circles, one inside (engulfed by) the other." There was no mention of what one was supposed to do with the third circle! No matter how a person answered these questions, the grader could always find a way to fail the test taker. Of course, most white southerners couldn't pass these tests, either. Many were illiterate, but that didn't seem to matter. If white voters were even asked to take a test, the graders made sure they passed. Sadly, these were the more subtle methods used to suppress the black vote. Would-be black voters were often threatened and sometimes killed. Preelection lynchings were common, reminding black citizens of what could happen to them if they challenged the system.

In the North, blacks were allowed to vote. Fewer lived there, so their voting power was not much of a threat to the control of white society. Even in the North, blacks were subject to a great deal of discrimination and segregation. Neighborhoods banned black families, schools were segregated, and many businesses posted "Whites Only" signs. Black people also found it very difficult to get good jobs.

The Supreme Court ruled in *Plessy v. Ferguson* (1896) that Jim Crow laws in the South were constitutional. According to the decision, this kind of discrimination was legal, as long as the facilities for blacks were equal to the facilities for whites. This was called the separate but equal doctrine.

ON THE ROAD TO FREEDOM

Long before the Selma march, African Americans had been fighting for their rights. In the early 1900s, blacks in cities around the South staged boycotts of segregated streetcars. These were largely unsuccessful, but they did draw attention to the problem of segregation. In 1909, black and white activists formed the National Association for the Advancement of Colored People (NAACP). The NAACP was formed primarily in response to nationwide violence against black communities. Its first initiative was an antilynching campaign. Over the years, the NAACP worked through the court system to end segregation and improve conditions for African Americans. The organization is still active—and effective—today.

During World War I (1914–1918), many African Americans moved from the rural South to the industrial North in the hopes of finding better jobs and less racism. For the most part, they were not welcomed. Many violent race riots broke out when blacks tried to protect their new homes from those who wanted to drive them back to the South. During the 1930s, however, African Americans increased their attempts to gain equality with white society. In 1936, the newly formed National Negro Congress brought together several civil rights groups to stage boycotts and protests against employment discrimination.

By the 1950s, sporadic protests and various organizations came together for a nationwide endeavor. The civil rights movement began in Montgomery, Alabama, in December 1955—almost ten years before the march from Selma to Montgomery. There, Rosa Parks refused to give up her bus seat to a white man. She was arrested, and the city's black community, led by Parks, Dr. King, Ralph Abernathy, and others, responded by organizing a citywide boycott of the bus system. The Montgomery bus boycott lasted 381 days. In the end, a US district court ruled bus segregation to be illegal. The Supreme Court soon validated this ruling, overturning *Plessy v. Ferguson* and invalidating the separate but equal doctrine. It was a huge win for civil rights and was the beginning of a movement that continues today.

FREEDOM RIDERS TRAVEL THE SOUTH

In 1957, buoyed by the success of the Montgomery bus boycott, sixty black ministers met in Atlanta, Georgia. They founded the Southern Christian Leadership Conference (SCLC). According to the King Institute, the goal of the SCLC was to "redeem the soul" of America through

Rosa Parks takes a mug shot after being arrested for refusing to give up her bus seat to a white man in December 1955.

nonviolent resistance. One of its earliest projects was to register as many black voters as possible for the 1958 and 1960 national elections. In voter education clinics around the nation, the SCLC spread the message that the route to a better life for African Americans was through the voting booth.

From May to November 1961, four hundred volunteer activists, both black and white, rode buses throughout the South to see if laws against segregation were being upheld. They were called Freedom Riders. For the most part, they traveled without incident. However, in South Carolina, some black Freedom Riders were beaten by white men when they attempted to use a bus station's "Whites Only" restroom. In Anniston, a small rural town in Alabama, the violence was much worse. There, Freedom Riders were met by a mob wielding baseball bats and throwing rocks. The mob slashed the tires of their bus. When the driver stopped to make repairs, the mob set fire to the bus. In Montgomery, an angry crowd used tire irons and baseball bats to beat Freedom Riders who were exiting their bus. When Freedom Riders arrived in Jackson, Mississippi, they were arrested, incarcerated, strip-searched, and beaten.

Throughout the years of the civil rights movement, activists faced violence and abuse. During the summer of 1964, many people, including college students from around

MURDER IN MEMPHIS

After the Montgomery bus boycott, Dr. Martin Luther King Jr. became the national leader, voice, and soul of the civil rights movement. In April 1968, he went to Memphis, Tennessee, to support sanitation workers who were striking for better wages and working conditions. He stayed in a motel, and on the evening of April 4, he stepped out on the balcony to address other civil rights leaders who were gathered in the parking lot below. At 6:05 p.m., he was fatally shot by a known racist, James Earl Ray. The nation was stunned. President Johnson declared April 7 to be a national day of mourning. On April 8, thousands of people, led by King's widow, Coretta Scott King, and other family members, marched through the streets of Memphis to honor the civil rights leader. They also showed their collective support for the striking sanitation workers. Long after his assassination, King's words and actions continue to inspire others to keep marching and to keep working to improve the world.

SCHWERNER   CHANEY   GOODMAN

Michael Schwerner (*left*), James Chaney (*center*), and Andrew Goodman (*right*) were murdered when they went to Mississippi to work for voter registration during 1964's Freedom Summer.

the nation, joined a program called Freedom Summer. They volunteered to help with voter education and registration in the South. It was a dangerous job. The Ku Klux Klan (KKK), a violent hate group, was waiting for them. On the first day of summer, three male volunteers went to inspect one of the churches that the KKK had burned down. One was black, James Chaney, and two were white, Andrew Goodman, and Michael Schwerner. But they never returned from the inspection. The men had been arrested and jailed. When released, a group of Klansmen was waiting for them. Their burned car was later found. Six weeks later, their bodies were found. All three had been shot, and Chaney had been severely beaten.

Incidents like this were all too common. Activists were not discouraged, though. They used these tragedies to convince the nation of the importance of the civil rights movement. They also encouraged others to use civil disobedience and nonviolent resistance in helping the nation change the way it treated African Americans.

CHAPTER TWO

TOO GREAT A BURDEN TO BEAR

On a January evening in 1956, a loud thud startled Coretta Scott King. It sounded as if someone had thrown a brick at the house. She was home alone with her infant daughter, while her husband, Dr. Martin Luther King Jr., was away at a meeting. He was planning and organizing the details of the Montgomery bus boycott. Mrs. King jumped up from watching television in the living room and ran to the back of the house. Her motherly instincts to rush to her baby, who was sleeping in a crib, saved her from injury. A bomb exploded, destroying the front porch, ripping a hole in the wall, and blowing out the front windows, which sprayed glass into the living room.

While at the meeting, Dr. King sensed that something was wrong. Someone came into the room and spoke quietly to Ralph Abernathy, one of the other civil rights leaders in attendance. Abernathy rushed downstairs and then returned with a worried expression. People turned to King and then to Abernathy. King asked what had happened, and Abernathy explained that King's house had been bombed. King rushed home, relieved to discover that his wife and baby daughter were uninjured.

DON'T GET PANICKY

The bombing of the King home was not unexpected. For weeks, Dr. King had been getting threatening letters and phone calls. In his memoir, *Stride Toward Freedom: The Montgomery Story*, he recalls some of these. One caller phoned King, called him a derogatory name, and threatened him, saying that King would be sorry for coming to Montgomery. King realized that at any time, his family could be taken away from him—or he could be taken from them. A few nights before his house was bombed, King sat at his kitchen table and prayed these words:

> *God, I am here taking a stand for what I believe is right. But now I am afraid. The people are looking to me for leadership, and if I stand before them without strength and courage, they too will falter. I am at the end of my powers. I have nothing left. I've come to the point where I can't face it alone.*

Dr. King then felt what he described as the presence of the divine. His fears melted away, and he knew that what he was doing was right. He was determined and ready to tackle whatever was coming his way. A few days later, King had to draw on his newfound courage and dedication to doing the right thing.

Moments after the bomb exploded on his front porch, a crowd gathered on the Kings' front lawn. There were more than one hundred of Dr. King's supporters, as well as white police officers. The crowd was angry and frightened, and many supporters carried weapons. King stepped out to speak to the crowd and immediately realized that this could quickly turn into a very volatile situation. He assured the crowd that his family was safe and urged his supporters to stay calm. In *Stride Toward Freedom*, he recalls saying, "Now let's not become panicky." He encouraged the onlookers to take their weapons home, since they couldn't fix the situation with additional violence. King insisted that violence must be challenged by nonviolence. He said, "We must love our white brothers no matter what they do to us."

King reminded them that law and order were what they believed in and that "he who lives by the sword shall die by the sword." This was the heart of the civil rights movement and the heart of King's philosophy of social change. He encouraged them to love their enemies but made it clear that he would not be intimidated. He said, "I want it to be known through the length and breadth of this land that if I am stopped, this movement will not stop. For what we are doing is right. What we are doing is just." Standing there on the porch that winter evening, King was powerful and inspiring. He truly was a great leader, leading by his example of how to face hatred with courage and love. But it wasn't easy, and he knew it wouldn't be easy for the others, especially in the hard days to come. King understood the power structure. He knew that if the protesters broke the law or became violent, they would be arrested and very likely killed by the police. White people had the power of the law and the courts on their side. Blacks would not change the situation by responding to violence in kind. It may have felt good at the moment, but retaliatory violence would only harm the civil right movement. They needed to convince the world that their cause was just. Years later, in an interview with Voice of America, civil rights lawyer Richard Cohen explained it by saying, "The violence was being perpetrated by the oppressors, not the oppressed and that was an incredibly powerful message and an incredibly important tool during the movement." King's commitment to nonviolence was not just practical. It was a decision driven by love.

Dr. Martin Luther King Jr. and his wife, Coretta Scott King, gather with supporters during the Montgomery bus boycott.

DECIDING TO LOVE

Dr. King was the minister of Montgomery's Dexter Avenue Baptist Church at the time of the Montgomery bus boycott. He was already a member of the executive committee of the NAACP and was active in civil rights work. Montgomery's black community chose him to be their leader, and he went on to become the primary leader of the civil rights movement until his death in 1968.

King had earned a degree in sociology from Morehouse College in Atlanta, Georgia, and a doctorate in theology from Boston University. While a student at Morehouse, he learned about Mahatma Gandhi, a social reformer who used nonviolent resistance to free India from British colonial rule in 1947. According to Morehouse College's King collection, King was also influenced by nineteenth-century American author Henry David Thoreau, who wrote the essay "On Civil Disobedience." King was especially impressed by Thoreau's idea of standing up against an evil system. King worked these ideas into his own philosophy of nonviolence. To understand King's approach, we must understand the way he saw violence. To him, poverty, racism, and militarism were all forms of violence. In a speech at an annual SCLC convention, later reproduced in a collection of King's writings titled *The Radical King*, King said, "Racism is a philosophy based on a contempt for life ... Inevitably it descends to inflicting spiritual or physical homicide upon the out-group."

Dr. King developed a set of principles to guide people in using nonviolence to bring about change. He said that nonviolence intends to defeat injustice and not people; it seeks to win friendship and understanding. Nonviolence chooses love, not hate. Hate is a violence to the

Mahatma Gandhi, Indian statesman and activist, inspires leaders around the world in the benefits and tactics of nonviolent resistance.

spirit as well as the body, and it damages the ones who hate as much as those who are hated. "Hate," said King, "is too great a burden to bear. I have decided to love." He believed that if one's goals were to create a better world, violence wouldn't work. In the same speech, King explained that "through violence you can murder a murderer, but you can't murder murder. Through violence you may murder a liar, but you can't establish truth. Through violence you may murder a hater, but you can't murder hate. Darkness alone cannot put out darkness; only light can do that."

Many of King's followers had trouble accepting the nonviolence doctrine. After all, they were being beaten and killed across the country. Certainly, they were victims of horrific violence, and responding with nonviolence would have seemed weak. To some, it even seemed to make them complicit in their oppression. But that is not at all what King meant by nonviolent resistance. Early in his career, in an address to the War Resister's League, King explained it like this:

The phrase "passive resistance" often gives the false impression that this is a sort of "do nothing method" in which the resister quietly and passively accepts evil. But nothing is further from the truth. For while the nonviolent resister is passive in the sense that he is

not physically aggressive toward his oppo-
nent, his mind and emotions are always
active, constantly seeking to persuade his
opponent that he is wrong. It is not passive
non-resistance to evil; it is active nonviolent
resistance to evil.

It's also important to understand that the tactics of nonviolent resistance are designed to be
disruptive. People can ignore marchers carrying
signs in the park. It's more difficult to ignore people who are sitting at a lunch counter and refusing
to leave. Most of the people who rode Montgomery's buses were black. When they stopped
riding, they stopped paying the fare. The bus
boycott cost the city of Montgomery a great deal
of revenue. Protests don't have to be loud and
aggressive to be effective. Quietly refusing to give
up your seat on a bus can be a very powerful way
to refuse to cooperate with an evil system.

MURDER IN CHURCH

People quickly saw the wisdom of Dr. King's ideas
and noted that the movement was peaceful. The
haters, however, continued with their violence. There
were times when the commitment to love and nonviolence was sorely tested. September 15, 1963, was

CÉSAR CHÁVEZ

Dr. Martin Luther King Jr. was not the only American leader to teach and use nonviolent resistance to achieve social change. Union leader and labor organizer Mexican American César Chávez used boycotts, marches, and several hunger strikes to bring attention to the terrible way that American farmworkers were being treated. In 1962, he founded the National Farm Workers Association, a union that advocated for better pay and working conditions for farmworkers. In 1968, Chávez led a national boycott of grapes, aimed at forcing grape growers to agree to contracts with grape pickers. These contracts would guarantee the workers better treatment, pay, and working conditions. It took many years, but his pressure on the grape growers was eventually successful. In 1970, twenty-six growers signed contracts agreeing to recognize the union and negotiate their demands. Chávez was also one of the first people to alert the world to the dangers pesticides posed to agricultural workers. He organized another boycott of grapes to pressure growers into remedying this problem.

In many ways, Chávez's labor movement was very much like the movement for civil

(continued on the next page)

(continued from the previous page)

rights for African Americans. He created coalitions of workers, students, and religious and community leaders. He staged huge marches and demonstrations that got the nation's attention. Through it all, he maintained his commitment to nonviolence. A famous photo of Chávez shows him sitting with Dolores Huerta, cofounder of the National Farm Workers Association, during a grape pickers' strike. He is standing under a portrait of Mahatma Gandhi.

César Chávez (*right*) and Dolores Huerta, cofounders of the National Farm Workers Association, sit under portraits of Robert Kennedy and Mahatma Gandhi as they discuss the grape boycott.

youth day at the Sixteenth Street Baptist Church,
a black church in Birmingham, Alabama. As wor-
shippers greeted each other and found their seats
upstairs, four young girls were downstairs in the
basement bathroom, checking their hair and making sure they looked pretty in their Sunday dresses
before going upstairs to the sanctuary to take part in
youth day. The girls never made it upstairs. A bomb,
planted under the steps of the church by KKK members, exploded. Addie Mae Collins (age fourteen),
Denise McNair (age eleven), Carole Robertson (age
fourteen), and Cynthia Wesley (age fourteen) were
killed in the blast. At least fourteen other children
were injured. Both the black community and the
white community were devastated and outraged.

For many blacks, the murder of these young girls
was a great test of their resolve to practice nonviolence and to counter hate with love. Many in the
black community decided that it was time to fight
back. Bobby Rush, a civil rights activist who is now a
US representative from Illinois, was interviewed later
by Voice of America. He explained how people in
the movement felt at the time. "I thought that Dr. King
was too milquetoast, too passive, and I didn't understand the power of nonviolence, so I didn't adhere
to his philosophy and turn the other cheek," recalled
Rush. King, however, kept his resolve and encouraged the rest of the movement to do the same. In his
eulogy for the murdered children, he encouraged the

This plaque at the Sixteenth Street Baptist Church in Birmingham, Alabama, honors the four girls murdered there in 1963. (Since this plaque was made, the murderers have been identified and punished.)

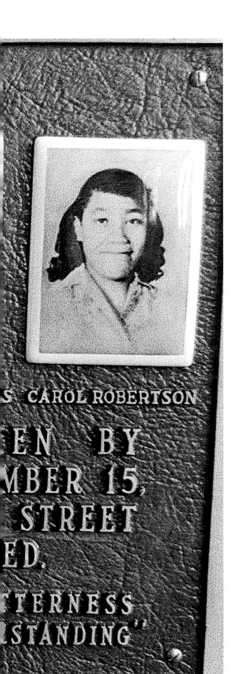

S CAROL ROBERTSON
EN BY
MBER 15,
STREET
ED.
TERNESS
STANDING"

community not to despair, to avoid bitterness, and to squelch the temptation to retaliate. He encouraged them to keep the faith for the white community, so that those who might act with discrimination would instead learn to value all humanity and behave accordingly.

King did not invent the idea of nonviolent resistance, nor did it die with him. Even when King himself was murdered, his followers remembered his teachings and stuck to his principles. This is true today as high school students organize marches or school walkouts to demand sensible gun legislation. We see it enacted when athletes "take a knee" during the national anthem to pro-

National Football League players link arms, and some kneel, during the singing of the national anthem to nonviolently protest police brutality and continued inequality of people of color in the United States.

test police brutality or to show support for their right to protest. We witness King's nonviolent approach when immigrants close their businesses for a day to demonstrate how much they contribute to the economy. These modern-day activists are expressing their disapproval of society in a way that brings harm to no one but instead brings a great deal of attention to problems and injustices.

CHAPTER THREE

THE POWER OF YOUTH

T he Birmingham church bombing was not the first time that young people made the national headlines during the civil rights movement. Plenty of them were behind the headlines, too. Young people are often the driving force behind social change. The protest against the Vietnam War (1955–1975) was driven largely by young people. The environmental movement is also powered by youth. Many of those involved in the Black Lives Matter movement are youths. Young people have a lot of energy and can bring about great changes in society—even before they are of age to vote. Their focus tends to be on local issues—and getting involved locally is undoubtedly the best way to make change happen.

The SCLC, NAACP, and other civil rights organizations had youth divisions. In 1960, a group of college students in North Carolina formed the Student Nonviolent Coordinating Committee (SNCC). The student-run group was founded on the principles of nonviolent social change, as exemplified by Gandhi and King. The SNCC was involved in

Students on college and university campuses around the nation, including many white students, were deeply involved in the civil rights movement.

the Freedom Rides and the Selma marches, as well as other similar actions during the 1960s.

RED AND YELLOW, BLACK AND WHITE

Not all young people who participated in the movement were African American. Joan Trump-auer Mulholland was one of many white youths who helped with the cause. When she was growing up in Arlington, Virginia, her Sunday school class sang the song "Jesus Loves the Little Children." Joan did not miss the hypocrisy of a segregated church singing the words "red and yellow, black and white, all are precious in his sight." She attended Duke University but dropped out to join the civil rights movement. Mulholland took part in many sit-ins and other demonstrations. When she was only nineteen years old, she was one of the Freedom Riders who was arrested and put in a penitentiary in Mississippi. Mulholland was the first white person to attend Tougaloo College, a historically black college in Jackson, Mississippi. Later, she became an officer in the SNCC.

In 1954, the Supreme Court case *Brown v. Board of Education of Topeka* declared that it was unconstitutional for states to send black students and white students to separate schools. In 1957, nine black students enrolled in a formerly all-white high school in Little Rock, Arkansas. The local chapter of the NAACP had recruited these nine brave youths to test the state's willingness to obey the new law. The students knew it would be difficult, but they may not have been prepared for what happened next. When they arrived for classes on the first day of the school year, they were met by angry protesters, shouting at them and calling them names. A white woman even spit on one of the girls!

Federal troops escort the Little Rock Nine off campus after a day of classes at the newly integrated Central High School in Little Rock, Arkansas.

The students could not enter the school, because the governor of the state, Orval Faubus, had ordered the Arkansas National Guard to block the door. The students were calm and determined. The incident made national headlines, and the students became known as the Little Rock Nine. Later that month, a federal judge ordered Governor Faubus to remove the National Guard. President Dwight D. Eisenhower sent in twelve hundred soldiers from the 101st Air Force Division of the US Army to escort the students to their classes. Throughout it all, these young people were dignified and committed to the cause. Though it took a while for the abuse and violence to end, the Little Rock Nine had made a big impression on the nation.

SUFFER THE LITTLE ONES

Ruby Bridges was just six years old when she became the first African American student to integrate into an elementary school in the South. Ruby was born in 1954, the same year as the *Brown v. Board of Education* ruling. Despite the dramatic events in Arkansas in 1957, southern schools were very slow to integrate. In 1959, Ruby attended an all-black kindergarten in her hometown of New Orleans, Louisiana. In 1960, a Federal Court ordered Louisiana to integrate its schools. In November of her first school year, Ruby began attending the formerly all-white William Frantz Elementary School. She was the only black child there. Every day, federal marshals escorted Ruby and her mother to school. They walked through a crowd of people who were shouting threats and racial slurs. When she got to school, only one teacher, Barbara Henry, was willing to teach Ruby. The two would sit in a classroom, just the two of them. Ruby ate lunch and spent recess alone. She was a brave little girl and didn't miss a single day that school year. Things gradually improved for Ruby and for the other black students who later attended William Frantz Elementary School and other formerly all-white schools.

Marilyn Luper was just eight years old when she had an idea that would change her hometown of Oklahoma City, Oklahoma. Her mother was the leader of the city's NAACP Youth Council. Marilyn was at a meeting one day when the discussion turned its attention to how to negotiate with down-town business owners. Meeting participants wanted to be allowed to sit wherever they wanted and be served in businesses and restaurants. In her inter-view for the Library of Congress Oral History Project, a grown Luper recalls that as a child, she suggested they go downtown to Katz Drug Store and, as she puts it, "just sit, just sit and sit until they served us." And that's what they did! Their brave actions led to the desegregation of the lunch counters in Oklahoma City.

SITTING-IN AND STANDING UP

Unlike in Oklahoma City, lunch counter sit-ins weren't as successful in Birmingham, Alabama. The city was one of the most segregated in the nation. The local movement, led by Reverend Fred Shuttlesworth, was doing its best but was not making much progress. In early April 1963, the SCLC partnered with local Birmingham civil rights leaders to bring national attention to the efforts to end segregation in the city. They called it the Birmingham Campaign. The national leaders trained volunteers in the methods of nonviolent protest

Ralph Abernathy (*foreground, left*) and Dr. Martin Luther King Jr. (*foreground, right*) are arrested in Birmingham after leading a march in the downtown business district in violation of a state ban on protests.

and expanded the demonstrations. The campaign increased its number of sit-ins at lunch counters and the public library and included a march on city hall, boycotts of downtown stores and businesses, and a voter registration drive.

On April 10, the city got a state court to ban the demonstrations. King and other leaders decided to ignore the ban. On Friday, April 12, King and several others were arrested for violating the ban. They were placed in solitary confinement, where they remained for nine days before being released on bond. While in jail, King wrote "Letter from a Birmingham Jail." It was a powerful response to white religious leaders who had called the demonstrations in Birmingham "unwise and untimely." In his letter, King pointed out that black people had waited long enough. He called out the white moderate who was, he wrote:

> More devoted to 'order' than to justice ... who constantly says: "I agree with you in the goal you seek, but I cannot agree with your methods of direct action"; who paternalistically believes he can set the timetable for another man's freedom.

White moderates were soon to get an even more powerful wake-up call, known as the Children's Crusade.

CHILDREN CRUSADING FOR CHANGE

SCLC leader James Bevel had an idea. He knew that many adults were afraid to join the protests, because they could not afford to lose their jobs—and were very likely to be fired if their white employers knew they had taken part. Instead, Bevel suggested the recruitment of students. King resisted the idea at first but eventually agreed, hoping that the presence of children marching for their rights would nudge the conscience of the nation. Bevel got to work. He and other civil rights leaders trained children and teenagers in the methods of nonviolent protest. The children were told they might be hit, spit on, or possibly arrested. While they were prepared for any scenario, the children learned that the only appropriate response to violence is no response.

On May 2, more than one thousand students headed not to school but to downtown Birmingham. Freeman Hrabowski was a twelve-year-old student at Birmingham's Ullman High School when he joined the march. He had heard Dr. King say that one of the reasons for the march was to gain the right to a better education. Many years later, Hrabowski told a journalist for The Root, "As a

Children and teenagers who participated in demonstrations in Birmingham are arrested and made to wait for a police van to take them to jail.

child, I was a fat nerd, but I loved school. I wanted to be a part of anything that would bring better education." At first, his parents didn't consent to let him go to the march. After thinking and praying about it, they agreed to let young Freeman participate. These kids were fighting for their future, and they were determined. Most were middle- and high-school-age students, but a few were as young as six years old. Every one mattered, and they joined what would later be called the Children's Crusade.

The marchers gathered downtown at the Six-teenth Street Baptist Church, where they were met by police. Hundreds of young people were arrested, put into paddy wagons and school buses, and hauled off to jail. More than six hundred were arrested that day. If the police thought that arresting hundreds of innocent youths would stop the protest, they were wrong. The next day, hundreds more arrived. Children were marching and singing "We Shall Overcome." This time, the police did more than just haul them off to jail. Eugene "Bull" Connor was commissioner of public safety for Birmingham and a white man who strongly opposed equal rights for blacks. When the children entered Kelly Ingram Park, across from the church, he ordered the police to disperse the children using clubs and police attack dogs. He ordered the fire department to spray them with powerful fire hoses. Nonetheless, the demonstrations continued. Inspired by the youth activists, adults began to join the protest, where they, too, faced snarling dogs and water blasting from fire hoses. Hrabowski later described the experience in a PBS documentary. Children were in jail, and some were crying. They were caged, being treated like animals. The older children tried to comfort the younger ones. Parents were on the outside, crying. Then Dr. King came by. He, too, had recently spent some time in Birmingham's jail.

A NEW CITY, A NEW COMMITMENT

In 1963, Birmingham, Alabama, was one of the most segregated cities in the nation. The viciousness of some of its leaders—those who tried to preserve that segregation—made a strong impression on the nation. However, things there have taken a turn for the better. Birmingham is a very different place now. Since 1979, every mayor has been an African American. The majority of its city council is made up of black members. In January 2017, the Birmingham City Council declared the city a sanctuary city. This means that Birmingham will enact polices to limit the federal government's power regarding immigration. The resolution states that the city "strives to be a community free of hostilities and aggressions and uphold the commitment to be a community free of prejudice, bigotry, and hate." The citizens of Birmingham, regardless of race and ethnicity, work hard to keep the memory of the civil rights movement alive. The Birmingham Civil Rights Institute is dedicated to preserving the memory of the movement and educating a new generation about civil rights. It's interesting to note, too, that the institute's windows look out across Kelly Ingram Park to the Sixteenth Street Baptist Church.

He told the children, "What you do this day will have an impact on children who've not yet been born." Even though they didn't fully understand, Hrabowski says the children realized that what they were doing was profound and important.

The goal of the Birmingham Campaign had been to attract national attention to the efforts to end segregation in Birmingham. When the national media began showing photographs and films of children being beaten, knocked down with fire hoses, and set upon by police dogs, all eyes were on the conflict. Millions of Americans were shocked out of complacency when they saw what was happening in Birmingham. US Attorney General Robert F. Kennedy sent his assistant for civil rights to negotiate a deal between Birmingham's black citizens and the city's leadership. On May 10, Dr. King and Reverend Shuttlesworth announced an agreement in which the city would desegregate lunch counters, restrooms, and water fountains. The city would also hire blacks to work in downtown businesses and develop a plan to improve the conditions of African Americans in the city. Birmingham released the protesters from jail. These efforts certainly did not stop racial discrimination in Birmingham. In fact, they ignited violence. A bomb damaged the motel where King, Abernathy, and other SCLC leaders were staying.

The Sixteenth Street Church bombing happened just four months later. However, the Birmingham Campaign was a turning point in the fight for civil rights. As Dr. King had hoped, the conscience of the nation had been awakened.

CHANGE MAKERS THEN AND NOW

The children of Birmingham set a fine example for adults and children across the country by upholding a nonviolent approach to violence. Yet protesting or activism doesn't have to be danger-ous to be effective, especially when social media helps spread important messages of activism. Children who want their voices to be heard can call on their families, teachers, and community mentors to advise them on how to make a differ-ence while staying safe.

Many of the people who were effective civil rights leaders—people who got things done and effected change for everyone—got their start in the movement when they were quite young. Many haven't stopped since. Freeman Hrabowski, the self-described "fat nerd" who loved education, grew up to become a mathematician and pres-ident of the University of Maryland, Baltimore County. John Lewis, the twenty-four-year-old who

On the steps of the Dexter Avenue Baptist Church in Montgomery, Alabama, the day before the Selma to Montgomery march, a young demonstrator holds a flag advocating for voting rights.

marched on the front lines on Bloody Sunday—
and got "cracked in the head" for his troubles
—now serves his home state of Georgia in Congress. Ruby Bridges remained a civil rights activist
into adulthood. In 1999, she established the Ruby
Bridges Foundation to promote tolerance and create change through education. Joan Trumpauer
Mulholland remained active in civil rights work.
The nonprofit Joan Trumpauer Mulholland Foundation carries on her work by educating children
about the civil rights movement, training them to
be activists for social justice. Many other young
civil rights leaders went on to successful careers
in law, politics, and education to continue the fight
for social justice.

CHAPTER FOUR

EYES ON THE PRIZE

· · · · · · · · · · · · · · ● ● ● ● ● ● ● · · · · · · · · · · ·

The Birmingham Campaign captured both the nation's attention and its conscience, and it is widely seen as a turning point in the struggle for equality for African Americans. As with any great movement, progress was incremental. There were many wins, as well as setbacks, along the way.

THAT'S AN ORDER

During World War II (1939–1945), many new jobs became available, including the production of airplanes, tanks, and other necessities for the war. African Americans faced discrimination and sometimes violence when they applied for these jobs. A group of black labor activists led by A. Philip Randolph threatened to organize a march on Washington if the government didn't fix the problem. In 1941—fourteen years before the Montgomery bus boycott—President Franklin D. Roosevelt signed Executive Order 8802. It

US president Franklin D. Roosevelt signed Executive Order 8802 in 1941 to prohibit discrimination in the defense industry and by federal agencies. It stands today.

prohibited discrimination based on race, creed, color, or national origin in the defense industries and in government. This was the same year that Rosa Parks began working for Maxwell Field (later known as Maxwell Air Force Base). While the military was still segregated at that time, this army air force base was integrated. Blacks and whites shared the facilities, and when Parks rode the base's trolley, she could sit wherever she pleased. She even chatted away with white passengers. It was a very different experience from the segregated city buses in Montgomery. When Parks left the base and rode the segregated Montgomery bus, she was forced to sit in the back, while white passengers rode up front. Further strides for integration were made when President Harry S. Truman signed Executive Order 9981. It desegregated the military in 1948. This order, along with Executive Order 8802, was a huge win for the civil rights movement, and it helped empower the black community for future activism.

The Montgomery bus boycott was ended by a district court ruling, *Browder v. Gayle* (1956). It made bus segregation illegal. The judges based their decision on the Supreme Court ruling *Brown v. Board of Education* (1954), which deemed segregation in schools to be illegal. It took a long time, though, to enforce these rulings. Activists worked together to put the force of the law behind efforts to end segregation across the United States. Three years later, Congress passed the Civil Rights Act of 1957. This legislation was not in itself very helpful, but it did show some political will at the national level to support civil rights legislation.

TELLING THEM ABOUT THE DREAM

Today's books and videos about the civil rights movement often focus on stories and images from two iconic events. The first was the Birmingham Campaign, with its lunch counter sit-ins and horri-fying confrontations in the park. The second was the August 1963 March on Washington for Jobs and Freedom, which took place just over three months later. It was an electrifying and uplifting action. In preparation, volunteers made eighty thousand boxed lunches, consisting of a cheese sandwich, a slice of pound cake, and an apple. As it turned out, the lunches weren't quite enough to feed the more than 250,000 people (some 60,000 of them white) who came from all over the country to march. To date, this was the largest protest in the nation's history.

The marchers gathered in front of the Lincoln Memorial, a powerful reminder of the nation's emancipation from slavery. The crowd was

People come from all over the nation to participate in the March on Washington for Jobs and Freedom in August 1963.

entertained by performers such as folk singer Bob Dylan and legendary gospel singer Mahalia Jackson. Many civil rights leaders made rousing speeches. The last speaker on the agenda was Dr. King. He had agreed to be the last so that some of the more established leaders could speak before the press got tired and quit covering the event. King was allotted four minutes. He began delivering the remarks that he and his speechwriter had prepared. King spoke of the significance of the march and of how black citizens were being denied what the Declaration of Independence (1776) promised, "life, liberty, and the pursuit of happiness."

Clarence B. Jones, King's speechwriter, described the events of that day in his book *Behind the Dream: The Making of the Speech That Transformed a Nation*. He details how Mahalia Jackson, who was standing on the podium near Dr. King, shouted, "Tell 'em about the dream, Martin; tell 'em about the dream." She was referring to a theme King had touched on in a few earlier talks to much smaller audiences. King glanced at Jackson, slid his notes aside, and raised his voice into that wonderful oratorical pitch for which he is now so famous. King then launched into what was one of the most powerful and moving speeches in American history. It has become known as the "I Have a Dream" speech. The full text can be found in many places, including the King Institute. According to that source, King said, using the call-and-response form so common in southern speeches and sermons:

> *I have a dream that one day this nation will rise up and live out the true meaning of its creed: "We hold these truths to be self evident: that all men are created equal."*
> *I have a dream that one day on the red hills of Georgia the sons of former slaves*

Dr. Martin Luther King Jr. waves to the crowd in front of the Lincoln Memorial as he delivers his speech at the 1963 March on Washington.

*and the sons of former slave owners will
be able to sit down together at the table
of brotherhood.*

King continued:

*I have a dream that my four little children will
one day live in a nation where they will not
be judged by the color of their skin but by
the content of their character.*

King's allotted four minutes turned into twelve.
No one seemed to notice or care. He was a master
of oratory, and on this day in 1963, the entire nation
heard him. The United States was no longer able
to turn away from the great injustice at its heart. If
the Birmingham Campaign had been the turning
point in the movement, the March on Washington
revealed its soul. And yet, there was still so much
more to do for the civil rights movement.

SOARING ORATORY GIVES WAY TO PRACTICAL POLITICS

President John F. Kennedy had been reluctant to
support stronger civil rights legislation. He agreed
in principle, but he didn't want to alienate white

WORKING TIRELESSLY FOR CIVIL RIGHTS

Dr. King definitely became the star of the March on Washington for Jobs and Freedom, but the person behind the scenes—the one who made the march happen—was Bayard Rustin. Rustin had worked with A. Philip Randolph to organize an earlier March on Washington in 1941. It was the fear of this march that motivated President Roosevelt to sign Executive Order 8802, ending discrimination in the defense industry and government. Rustin was happy with the order, but disappointed that the march had been called off. He worked tirelessly for civil rights, and twenty-two years later, got another chance with the 1963 March on Washington.

Rustin fell victim to discrimination for not only being an African American, but also for being gay. He did not hide his homosexuality, but frequently stayed in the background of the civil rights movement. Make no mistake, though, that Rustin, who was also a student of Gandhi's teachings on nonviolence, was one of the most influential leaders of the civil rights movement.

southern voters. He was convinced otherwise by the events in Birmingham and the nation's reaction to those events. Kennedy realized it was time to take action. In June 1963, he presented Congress with surprisingly comprehensive legislation. Getting that legislation passed, however, was another matter. One of the goals for the August 1963 March on Washington for Jobs and Freedom was to bolster support for that legislation. After the march, and King's monumental speech, soaring oratory gave way to practical politics. President Kennedy and Vice President

Civil rights leaders gather with President John F. Kennedy (*fourth from the right*) after the 1963 March on Washington. They successfully convinced the president of the need for civil rights legislation.

Lyndon B. Johnson met in the Oval Office with King, A. Philip Randolph, John Lewis, Roy Wilkins, Whitney Young, Floyd McKissick, and other civil rights leaders. The men discussed the legislation that was being worked out in Congress. Vice President Johnson explained the political complexities and gave the civil rights leaders some suggestions for building a coalition of support in Congress.

In November 1963, President Kennedy was tragically assassinated in Dallas, Texas. Lyndon Johnson then became president. In his first State of the Union Address in January 1964, Johnson pledged to support the proposed civil rights legislation and turn it into law. He wanted this congressional session to do more for the civil rights movements than any of the previous hundred sessions. Before becoming vice president, Johnson had been Speaker of the House of Representatives. The Speaker's job is to steer legislation through Congress. Johnson was a master at building coalitions, and he understood the complex operations of Congress. (He was also quite comfortable with bargaining, threatening, and bullying his opponents into doing what he wanted.) Those skills were sorely needed when it came to getting civil rights legislation past the strong opposition of congressional members from southern states. If anyone could do it, President Johnson could. On July 2, he signed into law the

Civil Rights Act of 1964. Richard Russell, a sena-
tor from Georgia who opposed the bill, is quoted
in the book *LBJ: Architect of American Ambition*
as saying, "You know we could have beaten John
Kennedy on civil rights, but not Lyndon Johnson."

The new Civil Rights Act of 1964 did quite a lot
for the minority populations. It prohibited discrimination in employment, in the workplace, in public
places, and in all agencies, organizations, and
institutions that received federal funds. Since most
schools received federal funds, this law made it
much more difficult for school systems to maintain
segregated classrooms. The new Civil Rights Act
ended separate water fountains and bathrooms.
In addition to outlawing discrimination based on
race, it outlawed discrimination based on color,
religion, sex, and national origin. According to a
transcript of the signing statement, available on
the website of the American Presidency Project,
President Johnson said, "We believe that all men
are entitled to the blessings of liberty. Yet millions
are being deprived of those blessings—not
because of their own failures, but because of
the color of their skin." Johnson noted that this
could not continue, saying, "Our Constitution, the
foundation of our Republic, forbids it. The principles of our freedom forbid it. Morality forbids it.
And the law I sign tonight forbids it." The president
also called on the country to get behind the effort

US president Lyndon B. Johnson shakes hands with Dr. Martin Luther King Jr. and gives him a ceremonial pen at the signing of the 1964 Civil Rights Act.

to make these news laws work, saying, "So tonight I urge every American to join in this effort to bring justice and hope to all our people and to bring peace to our land."

BACK TO THE STREETS

The Civil Rights Act of 1964 was a huge victory for African Americans. While it made discrimination and segregation illegal, it didn't make the discrimination disappear. The established political order—mostly made up of white politicians—was threatened by the protection of civil rights for African Americans. Racists pushed back, particularly in areas where blacks were the majority. For example, in Selma, Alabama, some racist politicians continued to make it very difficult for blacks to vote. In some places, states still charged a tax at the polls, which disenfranchised many southern blacks who could not afford to pay. States still required would-be voters to pass literacy tests before they could register to vote. When black voters were clearly able to pass a literacy test, election officials might ask them to recite the entire US Constitution or explain a complex point of law. White voters would not have been able to do this, either, but this task was not required of them. Local election officials used other, more subtle means to prevent African Americans from voting. They told black voters that they were at the wrong polling place or that they had arrived too late to vote. Polling places were often placed in neighborhoods far from where most blacks worked or lived. Voting hours were limited, making it difficult for them to get to the polls in time. Voting locations and times for black communities were changed frequently, which made things all the more confusing.

African Americans realized that the guaranteed access to a good education and employment, provided by the Civil Rights Act, was crucial for their freedom. They would be unable to protect those rights if they could not vote. Until they were able to vote, they would not be fully participating citizens of the United States. It was time to lace up those marching shoes once again. The march from Selma to Montgomery, the event that came to be known as Bloody Sunday, was meant to draw national attention to this problem. And it did. By this time, the nation was no longer willing or able to turn a blind eye to racism and discrimination. Congress had passed laws intended to make sure everyone had equal rights. Now the nation was called on to prove that it meant it.

Bloody Sunday happened in March 1965. Less than six months later, on August 6, President Johnson signed the Voting Rights Act of 1965. This law banned the use of literacy tests. (The Twenty-Fourth Amendment had made poll taxes illegal in national elections, and in 1966, the Supreme Court would rule poll taxes to be illegal in state elections.) Later, these rights would be expanded to cover Americans who do not speak English. Perhaps the most important aspect of the Voting Rights Act is that it required voting districts that had a history of voter suppression and racial discrimination to get federal approval—known as preclearance—before making any changes to their voting regulations or procedures. When the Voting Rights Act passed, there were only six African Americans serving in the US House

The State of the Union address, which the nation's legislators attend annually, featured more diversity than ever before in 2018.

of Representatives. The House's total membership at the time was 432. There were no African Americans serving in the Senate. By 1971, thirteen members of the House and one member of the Senate were black. By 2018, there were forty-eight African Americans in the House and three in the Senate. Forty-six were Hispanic or Latino; eighteen were Asian American, Indian American, or Pacific Islander American members; and two were Native American. The total congressional membership that year reached 541.

All these steps, all these wins—especially the Civil Rights Act and the Voting Rights Act—were extremely important for the civil right movement. They created a framework of law and precedent on which further gains could be made. These laws helped not only African Americans but also other people of color, immigrants, women, and members of the LGBTQ+ community. This was not the end, however. Much work remained in the fight to protect the rights of all Americans. That work continues today.

CHAPTER FIVE

STILL MARCHING

· · · · · · · · · · · · · ● ● ● ● ● ● ● ● · · · · · · · · · · ·

T he modern-day civil rights movement has expanded its goals from ending segregation and discrimination. It also encompasses reforming criminal justice, ending police violence toward blacks, and upholding the civil rights of underrepresented minorities living in the United States. Thanks to the hard work of activists and politicians during the early years of the movement, efforts and access to resources have made their work much more successful. But there are still great strides to be made. Change makers who are poised to take the movement to the next level are drawing lessons and inspiration from the civil rights leaders who came before.

ONE STEP BACK

For almost fifty years, the Voting Rights Act stood as a firm, legal barrier to those who tried to interfere with the right to vote. Then in 2013, a Supreme Court ruling, *Shelby County v. Holder*,

A protester in New York City takes a stand against police brutality and injustice that all too often targets people of color.

ec Mc Dade, 19,
ned, murdered by
ena police, 3/24/12

Jordan Baker, unarmed, 26,
murdered by Houston
police, 12/16/14

Manuel
killed by

Jaime Gonzalez, 15,
killed by Brownsville, TX
school police, 1/4/12

Corey Harris, 17,
murdered by Chicago
police, 9/11/09

k Dorismond, unarmed,
, murdered by NYPD,
3/16/2000

Amadou Diallo, unarmed, 23,
at 41 times and murdered by
NYPD, 2/4/99

cut the heart out of it. In this landmark case, Shelby County, Alabama, a largely white suburban county just south of Birmingham, challenged the preclearance requirement of the Voting Rights Act. The court did not rule that preclearance itself was unconstitutional. However, it did rule unconstitutional the formula used to determine to which districts this rule would apply. Chief Justice John G. Roberts Jr. explained the decision by saying that these formulas were no longer necessary. In his opinion for the majority, the chief justice wrote, "Our country has changed, and while any racial discrimination in voting is too much, Congress must ensure that the legislation it passes to remedy that problem speaks to current conditions." Many African Americans who were still having trouble casting their votes disagreed. Roberts was right about one thing, though—the country had changed. People who wanted to prevent blacks from voting had new techniques to suppress votes. This ruling made it legal for them to use those tactics.

The ink was hardly dry on the new ruling before voting districts that were now free from this oversight began to make changes to their registration and voting procedures. Many districts limited the hours that registration offices and polls were open in minority communities. Others enacted strict voter-ID laws, while at the same time restricting the hours and locations of offices that issue the required IDs. Many limited—or eliminated—the convenience of early voting and other measures designed to make it easier for people of color and those living in low socioeconomic neighborhoods to vote. The matter was brought to Congress. Civil rights activists are working to get legislation passed that will solve this issue and protect the right of all Americans to vote.

BRUTAL AUTHORITY

One of the tragic hallmarks of the Jim Crow South was violence against blacks. Lynchings, beatings, and other forms of violence and terrorism toward the black community were common. These acts were frequently overlooked by the authorities. Police violence was also an issue. The attacks by law enforcement officers in Selma and Birmingham caught the nation's attention,

#JusticeForEricGarner

color of change.org   JusticeForEricGarner.com

Despite a great deal of progress in civil rights in the past few decades, citizens still find that they have to take to the streets to demand justice.

but these were only a few examples of police brutality toward African Americans. The passage of the Civil Rights Act, while somewhat effective, couldn't prevent violence from continuing in the South and across the country. For example, police in Newark, New Jersey, severely beat a black cab driver after a traffic stop in 1967. In the ensuing riots, twenty-six people died, and many more were injured. Sadly, police brutality continues to be a problem today. Police officers kill an astonishing number of people in the

The National Guard confronts a group of angry protesters after the Newark race riots in Newark, New Jersey, in July 1967.

United States, a number that disproportionately represents African Americans or other people of color. Blacks make up 13 percent of the American population, but 31 percent of people killed by police are black.

The list of those black youths who have been killed by police in recent years is long. Eric Garner died after a New York City police officer put him in a choke hold during an arrest. John Crawford was fatally shot by police in Beavercreek, Ohio, while holding a toy BB gun in a Walmart store. Twelve-year-old Tamir Rice died after being shot by a policeman in a park who mistook his toy gun for a real one. Walter Scott was shot in the back by a police officer in Charleston, South Carolina, when he fled after being stopped for having a defective brake light on his car. And these are just a few examples. Many of these needless killings have spurred spontaneous and short-lived demonstrations. However, after police in Ferguson, Missouri, shot and killed an unarmed eighteen-year-old Michael Brown, local demonstrations grew into a national movement called Black Lives Matter. Organized and operated largely by young people, Black Lives Matter has brought worldwide attention to the fact that black people are more likely to be killed or abused by police than whites. The movement has put racism back on the national agenda.

BAKED-IN BARRIERS

In the United States, African Americans, especially men, are far more likely to be imprisoned
than their white neighbors. According to the
Bureau of Justice Statistics, African Americans
are jailed at three-and-a-half times the rate
of whites. Not only are they more likely to be
arrested and convicted of crimes, but also, when
convicted, they are typically given harsher sentences than whites who are convicted of similar
crimes. This is especially true for black males.
The reasons for this are complex and go beyond
racial bias (though there is still a great deal of
that, too). An example of this complexity involves
the laws that increase penalties for drug offenses
taking place near schools. These laws can have
the unintended consequence of targeting African
Americans, since studies show that black people
are more likely to live in densely populated urban
areas with many schools nearby. Another reason
for harsher sentences is that poor people—and
African Americans are statistically more likely
to be poor—can't afford high-quality legal representation when charged with crimes. Today's
civil rights workers and activists are attempting to
solve these and other problems within the criminal justice system. From police on the streets

to judges in the courts, these issues are com-
plicated and are the result of deeply embedded
factors in American society.

In 1934, the US government began a program
called the Federal Housing Administration (FHA).
The FHA guaranteed the money that banks loaned
to people to buy houses. Banks were more willing
to give home loans if they knew the government
would guarantee the loan. This made it possible
for many Americans to buy homes and is one of
the reasons for the enormous growth in the suburbs during the years that followed World War II
(1939–1945). The problem was that the FHA program was only for whites who wanted to live in
white communities. Loans were denied to African
Americans and to those white citizens who wanted
to buy homes in primarily black neighborhoods.
This effectively deprived many African Americans
of one of the most reliable routes to the middle
class: home ownership. It also promoted segregation, as blacks moved to the cities and whites to
the suburbs.

In 1968, Congress passed the Fair Housing
Act, making this kind of discrimination illegal.
However, the damage had been done. Much of
the wealth of the white middle class was in their
homes. Young whites often inherited houses from
the previous generation. As the nation prospered,
the value of those homes grew. People could sell

them for a profit and buy nicer homes. Or they could borrow against the value of their homes to send their children to college, start a new business, or invest in the businesses of others. The wealth created by home ownership could be used to create more wealth, thus allowing them to take advantage of educational and other opportunities. Black families who had been unable to buy homes during the postwar housing boom lost out on this chance for prosperity. As the white population moved to the suburbs, blacks were left in the city to rent homes in poorly funded school districts and with rapidly dwindling options for improving their lives. Frustrations mounted, and riots ensued. The summer of 1967 brought racial tension and violence in urban locations, namely Newark, New Jersey, and Detroit, Michigan. As a result, the US government commissioned a report on civil unrest in America. It was called the *Kerner Report* (1968), and it shone a light on unfair practices like those of the FHA. It explained how the institutions of white America contributed to the problems of the nation's black citizens. According to the *Kerner Report*:

> *Segregation and poverty have created in the racial ghetto a destructive environment totally unknown to most white Americans. What white Americans have never fully*

*understood—but what the Negro can
never forget—is that white society is deeply
implicated in the ghetto. White institutions
created it, white institutions maintain it, and
white society condones it.*

The *Kerner Report* clearly showed that there
were many ways to deny blacks the freedoms and
equality they had been promised. And some of
these methods were hardwired into both the history and economy of the nation. The report went
on to say that the riots were simply the natural
consequence of a society that was set up to privi-
lege one group at the expense of another. Policies
like FHA housing rules, mandatory sentencing
guidelines, and voter suppression are a part of
something known as structural racism or institu-
tional racism. They are policies and practices that
make it more difficult for African Americans—and
other minority groups—to prosper. Blacks no
longer have to sit in the back of the bus or use
separate restrooms, but they do face obstacles
that are just as serious, if not as obvious. These
are the kinds of problems that today's activists
are trying to solve. In some ways, these problems
are as challenging as facing down angry white
law enforcement officials with snarling dogs and
fire hoses.

BE CAREFUL OUT THERE

Reading about the civil rights movement can be inspiring, and there are plenty of ways you can safely get involved with social movements. Not all require taking risks. Writing letters to community and national leaders, signing petitions, sharing information with your friends, and talking with family members about the issues are all ways to help. If you do decide to take part in a march or protest, keep in mind these basic safety tips before you pick up a sign and head out to take action:

- Get permission from a parent or guardian before joining a protest. If you are interested in getting involved in a social movement, seek out an adult you trust for advice. This can include a family member, teacher, or minister.
- Get training. Be sure you know the basics of nonviolent resistance. If you are part of a planned march that has the proper permits to demonstrate in public spaces, then you aren't breaking the law. If you decide to break the law—as the

(continued on the next page)

(continued from the previous page)

marchers did in Birmingham in 1963—
realize that you may be arrested.
- If you're marching, be sure to carry water and
a fully charged cell phone.

During the 2017 National Day of Action Against Islamophobia & White Supremacy, young Canadians protest US president Donald J. Trump's travel ban on people from predominantly Muslim countries.

AROUND THE WORLD

In part, the awful events that took place in May 1963 in Birmingham, Alabama, convinced President Kennedy to change his mind and introduce civil rights legislation. His decision was also motivated by the world's reaction to the racial turmoil taking place in the United States. The appalling events in the South made the country look bad to its allies. Its enemies, particularly the former Soviet Union (now fifteen separate countries), used the racial conflict as evidence that democracy in the United States wasn't working. However, many people around the world who were also struggling for freedom and justice drew inspiration from the US civil rights movement.

In 1963, activists in England organized a non-violent protest inspired by the Montgomery bus boycott. They were responding to a bus company in the town of Bristol that refused to hire black or Asian drivers. The boycott was effective, and the bus company changed its policy after the March on Washington was broadcast internationally. Independence movements in several African countries both provided and received inspiration from the civil rights movement in the United States. In 1957, Dr. King and his wife, Coretta Scott King; black labor leader A. Philip Randolph;

In Los Angeles, California, protesters carry US and Mexican flags in a demonstration that supports immigrant rights.

and several other civil rights leaders attended Ghana's independence ceremony. Kenneth Kaunda, leader of the independence movement in Zambia, visited King in Atlanta in 1960. (Zambia was called Northern Rhodesia before it gained its independence from Britain in 1964.) Back in the United States, Mexican American and other Latino groups utilized the techniques of civil rights leaders to demand economic and social justice and protection of their right to vote.

The civil rights movement brought more change and

improvement to the lives of African Americans than anything since the end of slavery.
These accomplishments did not come about by
random protest. Organized, planned, and coor-
dinated efforts were behind the success of every
endeavor. A commitment to nonviolent resistance
and an unwillingness to give up eventually brought
about great advances. Today, another dedicated
generation is building on those advances and
refusing to stop marching in pursuit of equality
for all.

TIMELINE

1865 The Thirteenth Amendment to the US Constitution is ratified, ending slavery.

1868 The Fourteenth Amendment to the US Constitution is ratified, turning former slaves into citizens.

1870 The Fifteenth Amendment is passed into law, giving black men the right to vote.

1896 In *Plessy v. Ferguson*, the Supreme Court rules that segregation is legal in public facilities, as long as they are equal in quality for all citizens.

1954 The Supreme Court rules that school segregation is illegal in *Brown v. Board of Education of Topeka*.

1955 The civil rights movement begins when Rosa Parks refuses to give up her seat on a Montgomery bus, giving rise to the Montgomery bus boycott in Montgomery, Alabama.

1956 Bus segregation is determined to be illegal, and the Montgomery bus boycott ends.

1957 President Dwight D. Eisenhower signs the Civil Rights Act of 1957. This new law brings an end to segregation in public places and employment discrimination.

1963 The Birmingham Campaign and the Children's Crusade bring national attention to the racial problems in the South.

1963 A quarter of a million people march on Washington, DC, demanding civil rights for African Americans.

1963 Four young black girls are killed in a racially motivated bombing of a church in Birmingham, Alabama.

1964 The Civil Rights Act of 1964 is signed into law by President Lyndon B. Johnson.

1965 The Voting Rights Act of 1965 becomes law, making it illegal for racial discrimination to prevent citizens from voting.

1968 Dr. Martin Luther King Jr. is assassinated in Memphis, Tennessee.

1968 The Fair Housing Act is passed, prohibiting discrimination against those of any race, religion, nationality, or gender from buying, renting, or financing housing.

action A planned demonstration or protest intended to draw attention to or make a point about social issues.

boycott A refusal to conduct business with or buy products from a business or organization, in order to express disapproval or attempt to change policy.

coalition An alliance, often temporary, of groups that work together to achieve a particular end.

complacency Satisfaction due to the ignorance of a serious issue or dangerous situation.

disenfranchise To deny someone the right to vote.

federal Having to do with the central government of the United States, rather than state or local governments.

iconic Relating to a symbol or representation of something, such as an idea, event, or historical period.

incremental Occurring in small pieces or steps.

legislation A group or set of laws.

lynch To murder someone, usually by mob hangings.

militarism A belief that the federal government should use a strong military to defend its interests.

milquetoast A timid or submissive person.

nightstick A club or truncheon sometimes used by police officers.

oratory The art of public speaking, especially with eloquence and passion.

penitentiary A state or federal prison for those who have committed serious crimes.

precedent An example or guide to be followed in similar situations occurring in the future, especially in regard to legislation.

reverend A title for members of the clergy.

segregation The practice of separating people according to racial differences.

sit-in A protest or demonstration in which activists sit in a public place, such as a segregated lunch counter or city hall, and refuse to leave until their demands are met.

unconstitutional Something, such as a law, that is not in keeping with the dictates set forth by the US Constitution.

FOR MORE INFORMATION

American Civil Liberties Union (ACLU)
125 Broad Street, 18th Floor
New York, NY 10004
(212) 549-2500
Website: https://aclu.org
Facebook and Twitter: @aclu
Instagram: @aclu_nationwide
YouTube: acluvideos
This organization, founded in 1920, has spent
    almost a century defending and protecting
    the individual rights and liberties that are
    guaranteed by the Constitution of the United
    States.

Birmingham Civil Rights Institute (BCRI)
520 Sixteenth Street North
Birmingham, AL 35203
(866) 328-9696
Website: https://www.bcri.org
Facebook: @bcri.org
Twitter and Instagram: @bhamcivilrights
A museum and research center situated directly
    across from the Sixteenth Street Baptist
    Church in Birmingham, Alabama. It focuses
    on keeping alive the memory of the civil rights
    movement and working to help each new gen-
    eration build a better future.

Brennan Center for Justice at NYU School of
Law (BCJ)
120 Broadway, Suite 1750
New York, NY 10271
(646) 292-8310
Website: https://www.brennancenter.org
Facebook and Twitter: @BrennanCenter
Instagram: @brennancenter
Email: brennancenter@nyu.edu
This nonpartisan law and policy institute supports
the values of democracy and equal justice for
all. Protection of voting rights and campaign
finance reform are among its goals.

Canadian Civil Liberties Association (CCLA)
90 Eglinton Avenue E., Suite 900
Toronto, ON M4P 2Y3
Canada
(416) 363-0321
Website: https://ccla.org
Email: mail@ccla.org
Facebook and Twitter: @cancivlib
YouTube: @CanCivLib
An organization fighting for the civil liberties and
human rights of all Canadians.

Congress of Black Women of Canada—Ontario
Region
c/o Congress of Black Women of Canada—Missis-
sauga Chapter

4983 Rathkeale Road
Missussauga, ON L5V 2B3
Canada
(866) 986-2292
Website: http://www.cbwc-ontario.com
Email: cbwontarioinc@gmail.com
This national nonprofit works to help create better
    living conditions for black Canadian women
    and their families.

Leadership Conference on Civil and Human Rights
1620 L Street NW, Suite 11000
Washington, DC 20036
(202) 466-3311
Website: https://civilrights.org
Facebook: @civilandhumanrights
Twitter: @civilrightsorg
YouTube: @LCCREF
This is a diverse coalition of over two hundred
    organizations. Its goal is to protect the civil and
    human rights of Americans.

Southern Christian Leadership Conference (SCLC)
320 Auburn Avenue NE
Atlanta, GA 30303
(404) 522-1420
Website: http://nationalsclc.org
Facebook and Instagram: @nationalsclc
Twitter: @nationalSCLC
Email: contact@nationalsclc.org

An active civil rights organization born of the Montgomery bus boycott.

Southern Poverty Law Center (SPLC): Teaching Tolerance Project
400 Washington Avenue
Montgomery, AL 36104
(888) 414-7752
Website: https://www.splcenter.org/teaching -tolerance
Facebook: @SPLCenter
Twitter: @Tolerance_org
Instagram: @teaching_tolerance
A project of the SPLC, with an emphasis on social justice and inclusiveness, Teaching Tolerance provides teaching resources and information to help schools prepare students to be active and effective members of a diverse democracy.

FOR FURTHER READING

Baldwin, James. *The Fire Next Time.* New York, NY: Vintage Books, 1962.

Coates, Ta-Nehisi. *Between the World and Me.* New York, NY: Spiegel and Grau, 2015.

Curtis, Christopher Paul. *The Watsons Go to Birmingham—1963.* New York, NY: Random House Children's Books, 1995.

Gay, Kathlyn. *Activism: The Ultimate Teen Guide.* Lanham, MD: Rowman and Littlefield Publishing Group, 2016.

Mortensen, Lori. *Voices of the Civil Rights Movement: A Primary Source Exploration of the Struggle for Racial Equality.* North Mankato, MN: Capstone Press, 2015.

Shoup, Kate. *The Freedom Riders: Civil Rights Activists Fighting Segregation.* New York, NY: Cavendish Square Publishing, 2018.

Spence, Kelly. *Martin Luther King Jr. and Peaceful Protest.* New York, NY: Cavendish Square Publishing, 2017.

Staley, Erin. *Martin Luther King Jr. and the Speech That Inspired the World.* New York, NY: Rosen Publishing, 2015.

Thomas, Angie. *The Hate U Give.* New York, NY: Balzer + Bray, 2017.

Thompson, Laurie Ann. *Be a Changemaker: How to Start Something That Matters.* New York, NY: Simon Pulse, 2014.

BIBLIOGRAPHY

Burrow, Rufus, Jr. *Martin Luther King, Jr., and the Theology of Resistance.* Jefferson, NC: McFarland and Company Publishers, 2015.

Edelman, Peter. "50 Years Later: Why We Must Remember the Civil Rights Movement." Moyers & Company, July 10, 2014. http://billmoyers.com.

Gilmore, Kim. "The Birmingham Children's Crusade of 1963." Biography, February 14, 2014. https://www.biography.com.

Holmes, Marian Smith. "Freedom Riders, Then and Now," Smithsonian.com, February, 2009. https://www.smithsonianmag.com/history/the-freedom-riders-then-and-now-45351758.

Johnson, Lyndon B. "195—Remarks Upon Signing the Civil Rights Act." American Presidency Project, April 11, 1968. http://www.presidency.ucsb.edu/ws/index.php?pid=28799.

Jones, Clarence B. *Behind the Dream: The Making of the Speech That Transformed a Nation.* New York, NY: St. Martin's Griffin, 2011.

Jones, Josh. "Take the Near Impossible Literacy Test Louisiana Used to Suppress the Black Vote (1964)." Open Culture, July 23, 2014. http://www.openculture.com/2014/07/literacy-test-louisiana-used-to-suppress-the-black-vote.html.

King, Martin Luther, Jr. "Address at the Conclusion of the Selma to Montgomery March." Martin Luther King, Jr. Research and Education Institute, March 25, 1965. http://kingencyclopedia.stanford.edu.

King, Martin Luther, Jr. "Address at the Thirty-Sixth
    Annual Dinner of the War Resisters League."
    Martin Luther King, Jr. Papers Project,
    February 2, 1959. http://okra.stanford.edu.
King, Martin Luther, Jr. "I Have a Dream." Speech,
    Washington, DC, August 28, 1963.
King, Martin Luther, Jr. *Stride Toward Freedom:
    The Montgomery Story.* Boston, MA: Boston
    Beacon Press, 2010.
King, Martin Luther, Jr., and Cornel West (ed.). *The
    Radical King.* Boston, MA: Beacon Press, 2015.
Milloy, Courtland. "Remembering the Everyday
    Heroes of the Civil Rights Movement." *Washing-
    ton Post*, August 27, 2013. https://www
    .washingtonpost.com.
National Advisory Commission on Civil Disorders.
    Kerner Report. Princeton, NJ: Princeton Univer-
    sity Press, 2016.
O'Donnell, Michael. "How LBJ Saved the Civil
    Rights Act." *Atlantic*, April 2014. https://www
    .theatlantic.com.
Perry, Chiara. "Birmingham City Councilors
    Approve Sanctuary City Resolution." Birming-
    ham City Council, February 2, 2017. http://
    www.birminghamalcitycouncil.org.
Simkins, Chris. "Nonviolence Was Key to Civil
    Rights Movement." Voice of America, January
    20, 2014. https://www.voanews.com.
Stewart, Denise. "Children's March 1963: A Defiant

Moment." *Root*, May 1, 2013. https://www
.theroot.com/childrens-march
-1963-a-defiant-moment-1790896253.
Sugrue, Thomas J. *Sweet Land of Liberty: The
Forgotten Struggle for Civil Rights in the North*.
New York, NY: Random House, 2008.
Woods, Randall B. *LBJ: Architect of American
Ambition*. New York, NY: Free Press, 2006.

INDEX

ABOUT THE AUTHOR

Avery Elizabeth Hurt is the author of numerous books for children and young adults. She grew up in various places around the South and has seen many instances of racial injustice. She is happy to say that the South is a much different place from what it was during her childhood. She currently lives in Birmingham, Alabama, where the fire department now uses its fire hoses only to put out fires.

PHOTO CREDITS